A BOY

BURIED TREASURE

FANTAIL PUBLISHING,
AN IMPRINT OF PUFFIN ENTERPRISES

Published by the Penguin Group
27 Wrights Lane, London W8 5TZ England

Viking Penguin Inc., 375 Hudson Street, New York, New York
10014, USA.
Penguin Books Australia Ltd. Ringwood, Victoria, Australia.
Penguin Books Canada Ltd., 2801 John Street, Markham,
Ontario, Canada LR3 1BA.
Penguin Books (NZ) Ltd., 182-190 Wairau Road Auckland 10
New Zealand.
Penguin Books Ltd., Registered Offices: Harmondsworth,
Middlesex, England.

First Published by The Berkley Publishing Group 1990
First Published in the UK by Penguin Books 1990

10987654321

0140 903119

A BOY'S BEST FRIEND

A Novel by Nancy E. Krulik

Based on the Al Burton Production LASSIE

Adapted from the episode "A DOG AND HIS BOY"

Written by Bud Wiser

CHAPTER 1

"Will, think fast!" Chris McCulloch shouted to his ten-year-old son as he kicked the old leather soccer ball across the freshly cut grass of the front lawn. The ball flew off in the boy's direction. With a look of determination on his face, and one swift, strong kick, Will drove the ball right back to his father. Mr. McCulloch ran for the ball but he overstepped it and, as he kicked at the air, he fell to the grassy ground with a loud thud!

"Good move, Dad," Will said with a giggle, his blue eyes flashing. "You learn that from my soccer videocassettes?"

"Very funny." Mr. McCulloch grinned at his son as he got up and brushed himself off. "Now, let's get to practice. We're late!"

Eagerly, Will grabbed his black soccer shoes with the sharp cleats from the porch—his parents wouldn't let him wear his cleats on the lawn; "They make too many holes in my lawn," his mother was fond of saying—and ran to the family's black 4X4. He hopped in the front passenger seat, buckled up, and waited in anticipation.

Saturday soccer practice was Will's favorite time of the week. Although the McCullochs had moved to Glen Ridge from San Diego just a few months before, Will was already a first string player on his soccer team. The rest of the family was settling in to life in their new town, too. Will's dad, Chris, owned a construction company which had gotten some important contracts to build new shopping centers in the area. Will's mother, Dee, had started a personnel business and she was working closely with local business owners to provide them with talented employees. In a very short time, Dee already had more clients than she could handle. It was because of the people they met through Dee's business that Will's parents had made so many new friends in Glen Ridge.

But when it came to new friends, Will's fourteen-year-old blond-haired blue-eyed sister, Megan, had them all beat. She was already a member of the cheerleading squad at the local high school (even if it was only as the team mascot), and she was a star member of the photography club. Chances were, if the family phone rang after three o'clock, it was for Megan.

But the member of the McCulloch family who liked living in Glen Ridge the best was Lassie, the family's beautiful, purebred, white and golden pet collie. When the family lived in San Diego, Lassie spent a lot of time cooped up inside the McCulloch family's small house or chained up outside in the yard. The old city neighborhood was too busy to allow even a dog as smart and careful as Lassie to run around without a leash. But here in suburban Glen Ridge, where there were fewer cars and almost no strangers, Lassie was free to play with other dogs and run around the neighborhood.

Lassie loved to run. She loved the feel of the wind blowing through her fur and the sun warming her bones as her bushy tail wagged happily behind. The McCullochs never worried about Lassie running around in the new neighborhood. She knew not to wander carelessly in the streets, not to travel too far, and not to bother anybody. Besides, thanks to characteristics she inherited from her wolf ancestors, Lassie had a terrific sense of smell and an amazing sense of hearing, so she never had any problem tracking her way home. And somehow, Lassie always knew when it was time to come home. Because she was so responsible, the McCullochs trusted Lassie to do as she pleased. So, the neighbors got used to seeing the proud collie trot past their houses on her daily morning run.

Now, as Lassie watched Will and his father get into the big family 4X4, she got very excited. She wanted to go along for the ride. There was nothing Lassie liked more on a bright sunny day than a ride in the family car.

"Ruff, ruff, ruff!" she barked excitedly as she left the brightly colored flowers she had been sniffing and came racing across the lawn to the driveway, wagging her tail in a joyous frenzy.

When she reached the car, Lassie jumped up and down, turning in circles with excitement. Finally, she lifted her head and pressed it against the open window, panting. Then she pushed her face in the car and licked Chris McCulloch right on his bushy brown moustache! Chris stuck his hand out of the window and scratched the triangle of snow-white fur on Lassie's long, pointed nose.

"Sorry, Lassie," he told her. "You can't come this time. We're saving you for the playoffs!" he joked with the collie.

With that, Mr. McCulloch started the motor, and Lassie jumped out of the way. She walked over to the grass and watched sadly as the car pulled out of the driveway.

As soon as the car was out in the street, Lassie followed it for a while. She barked loudly at Will and his dad. But the car could outrun even the strong legs of a collie, and soon the shiny chrome of the 4X4 was out of sight. Finally, Lassie gave up, turned and trotted back up the street to the house.

Lassie was about to head inside the house to see if Megan wanted her to pose for some photographs, or if Dee McCulloch wanted to go for a walk. But before she could reach the house, something in the air made Lassie stop suddenly on the driveway. She lifted her long, narrow head and looked out over the neighborhood. Her bright, sharp eyes smarted as the glaring morning sun bounced off the cream-colored sidewalk and into her face. Lassie had the sudden sensation that something was very, very wrong. It wasn't something she could see or smell or hear, it was more like a sixth sense, an intuition. Lassie had gotten these sensations before. She was never sure where the feelings came from, but she knew they were never wrong. Someone was in trouble, and it was up to her to help!

In a split second, Lassie was running at top speed. She wasn't quite sure where she was headed, but she was certain that if she kept running, she was sure to find out where the trouble was. The town wasn't very big, after all. The neighborhood turned into a blur as her strong legs carried her past the brick houses, over the carefully mowed lawns, and around the bright green trees and colorful spring flowers. Her paws barely touched the sidewalk as she moved, darting in and out of the small side streets.

Before long, Lassie found herself in the center of town where the shops and restaurants were. Lassie dodged the people on the sidewalk as she kept her eyes peeled for any sign of trouble. Her pointed ears were tilted slightly forward, listening for the slightest cry for help.

Then she heard it—the call for help she had suspected! It came in the form of a small, weak, whimpering cry. Lassie cocked her head. The sound was coming from a tiny alleyway that was wedged between the backs of two warehouses. Lassie stopped short at the entrance to the alley. Her heart pounded against the clean white ruff of her chest as she stood very still, ears perked, listening again for the tiny whine.

"Ah, ah, ah," the little voice murmured again. This time the cry was even weaker than before.

The call was coming from a stack of old crates at the back of the alley, behind one of the warehouses. Lassie looked down the alley. It was filled with spilled garbage, tin cans, and broken glass. The stench of rotted meat and spoiled milk hung heavily in the air. A rusty loading dock stood between the pile of crates and the garbage dumpsters.

At first, Lassie was tempted to leave. But then the tiny whimper started up again. "Ah. Ah."

With a look of determination on her face, Lassie hopped up on the loading dock and padded cautiously over to the crates. She moved very quietly so as not to frighten the whimpering creature that was hidden there.

Lassie sniffed around the crates a few times. Finally, she poked her nose between the slats in a small crate at the bottom of the pile. What she saw made her heart heavy with sadness. There, lying in a nest of old newspapers was a tiny, scrawny, dirty, abandoned puppy. The puppy's muddy brown hair was matted and tangled, his gray eyes were clouded and sad, and his ears were flopped close to his head.

Lassie lifted her head and tilted it into the crate to get a better look at the poor dog. She was about an inch from the pup. Then she bent over and looked him straight in the eye.

Taking one look at the regal, long-nosed dog that was staring down at him, the puppy became terrified. He struggled to his feet and huddled in the corner of the crate. The poor stray shook with fear as Lassie nuzzled his floppy ear with her long, wet nose. Lassie, sensing that the little fellow was still afraid, moved away from the puppy. Standing at a safe distance, she wagged her tail and let out a happy bark. It was her way of saying "I want to be your friend."

Lassie waited for the puppy to answer her, but

he didn't make a sound. He was far too weak and hungry to understand. Still, Lassie wasn't going to give up so easily. She moved closer to the puppy. Craning her neck to reach him, Lassie stuck out her rough pink tongue and licked the poor little stray on the top of the head. But instead of wagging his tail, the puppy became even more petrified of the bigger dog and buried himself in the pile of newspapers.

The puppy had lived his entire short life alone. He never had a chance to learn to trust. Nothing Lassie could do was going to convince him that she was a friend who only wanted to help him.

Lassie looked over at the puppy and realized that even if she could get him to trust her enough to follow her home, he was too weak to make the trip across town to the house. No, this little fellow was going to have to stay put in his crate in the alley until Lassie could bring someone from her family to help.

Wagging her tail, Lassie let out one more bark.

"I'll be back with help," she tried to tell the small lonely stray. But deep inside, she knew he didn't understand. She would have to hurry—the little guy was not well at all!

She darted back to the McCullochs at top speed.

CHAPTER 2

By the time Lassie reached home, Megan was already off at the mall shopping with friends. And even though it was Saturday, Dee McCulloch was busy working at her desk in the family room. Sitting beside Dee was a casually dressed woman in her mid-thirties named Nancy Shaw. Mrs. Shaw was Dee's newest business client. Like the McCullochs, Nancy Shaw was new to Glen Ridge and so far Dee was the only person she'd met. On the other side of the room sitting in the overstuffed easy chair was Mrs. Shaw's twelve-year-old son, Neil.

Dee was trying to find a job for Nancy Shaw. Papers were scattered all over the desk and large manilla folders lay open on the plush carpet.

Finding the right job for Nancy Shaw wasn't an easy task. Nancy didn't want to be away from

Neil for any long period of time during the day. Neil wasn't an ordinary boy. He had a lot of problems. Mostly he just sat by himself, staring out into space. He never hugged anyone, or smiled. He never played or laughed with other kids. He never spoke to anyone and he didn't look people in the eye when he was spoken to. He never showed any emotion except, on occasion, fear. It was as though Neil was alone in his own world, a world which he wouldn't leave or allow anyone to enter.

That was why Mrs. Shaw wanted to spend as much time with her son as possible. She knew Neil needed extra love and attention to break through the imaginary wall he had built up around himself.

"We just have to find something where you can set your own hours, Nancy," Dee said, toying with her short brown hair as she looked through her files for a company that would let someone do just that.

"That's all?" Mrs. Shaw asked sarcastically. "Do you get a lot of calls for jobs like that?"

"Actually, you're the first one I've had who's needed a job like this," Dee admitted. Nancy Shaw's face fell in a hopeless frown. "But there's a first time for everything!" Dee quickly added.

Nancy Shaw walked lovingly over to the easy chair where her son, Neil, sat absolutely still, his feet set firmly on the floor and his hands gripping the chair arms. She rubbed his back gently, but the boy didn't move.

"I don't want to be away from Neil eight hours a day," she said softly.

"You've got a great mom there, Neil," Mrs. McCulloch said, smiling confidently. "We're going to find her a terrific job!"

"Arf! Arf! Arf!" Just then Lassie came bursting into the family room, barking with all her might. It was her "help, there's an emergency" bark. Lassie didn't use the bark often. But right now she needed to make Mrs. McCulloch understand that she needed her help right away for the hungry stray puppy in the alleyway.

The loud noise and sudden movement of the collie startled Neil. Instinctively, he grabbed his mother's arm and held on tight, turning his head from the dog.

"Lassie! No! Lassie down!" Mrs. McCulloch ordered. She was too concerned about Neil's frightened reaction to the bark to recognize that the collie's loud, constant call was not Lassie's ordinary "hello, I'm home" bark.

No matter what, when one of the family members gave her an order, Lassie always did as she was told. So now, even in her panic, she lay down on the floor so that her stomach touched the thick carpet. Then she stretched out her front legs and put her head on her paw. Lassie may have laid down, but she didn't calm down. Looking up at Mrs. McCulloch with her soft brown eyes, Lassie began to whimper.

Mrs. McCulloch ignored her. "I'm sorry, Neil," she apologized. "Lassie's just excited."

Neil held tight to his mother's arm, his head buried in her side.

"It's not her fault," Mrs. Shaw explained. "Neil's absolutely terrified of dogs."

Dee understood. She knew an easy way to get Lassie into another room. "Lassie, in the kitchen," Mrs. McCulloch ordered the dog. "Come on, get a biscuit," she added in a tempting tone.

A biscuit wasn't what Lassie wanted just then. What she wanted was someone to go with her to the alley. But Lassie always obeyed, so she silently followed Mrs. McCulloch into the kitchen.

Reaching way back into the top kitchen cabinet, Mrs. McCulloch brought down a bag of Lassie's favorite dog biscuits. She took one out of the bag and put the rest on the kitchen table. Then, bending down, she scratched Lassie's soft white belly and handed her the biscuit.

"That's a good girl," Dee said in soft, even tones. "I know it's not your fault. Neil just doesn't know you yet."

Lassie took the biscuit in her mouth and chewed it slowly and without enthusiasm. As Mrs. McCulloch got up to leave the kitchen, Lassie let out a loud, sharp bark. She just had to get Dee's attention!

But Mrs. McCulloch misunderstood. She didn't realize it was a bark for help. She thought Lassie was being greedy.

"No, one biscuit is all you get," she said as she left the kitchen and returned to her guests.

Lassie started to go after her, but she got a better idea. In a flash, Lassie grabbed the bag of biscuits on the table in her mouth. Then, walking out into the front hall, she looked around, checking to make sure the coast was clear. She didn't want to get caught taking the whole bag of biscuits. When she was sure no one was looking, Lassie tiptoed quietly out the open front door, clutching the bag of biscuits tightly between her teeth.

As soon as she got outside, Lassie took off as fast as a flash of lightning. This time Lassie didn't have to wonder where she was going. Her keen sense of direction told her exactly how to reach the alley. She even took a shortcut to save time. The running collie was a beautiful sight as she galloped at top speed, leaping over fences as though she could fly.

When she got to the alley, Lassie didn't take the time to stop to catch her breath. Instead, she walked quickly through the trash and up on to the loading dock to get to the puppy's hideout. What she saw there made her very sad. The starving, lonely puppy looked weaker than ever. He couldn't even muster up the strength to be afraid of Lassie. It took all of his strength just to look up at her with helpless dull gray eyes.

Gently, Lassie opened her strong jaws and dropped the bag of biscuits next to the stray. The bag opened, and seven brown, bone-shaped doggie biscuits fell out into the crate. The puppy looked curiously at the food for just an instant. Then, as though he suddenly remembered what to do with food, the puppy opened his mouth and with his sharp white teeth began to devour the biscuits as quickly as he could.

As soon as the puppy had eaten three of the biscuits, he began to come to life. He stood on his uncertain legs, shook his tiny body, and stretched. With a quiet yelp, he walked over to the side of the crate where Lassie stood, patiently waiting. The little mutt looked at Lassie and cautiously wagged his tail. Lassie wagged back and let out a gentle "woof" in friendship.

Nudging with her wet black nose, Lassie helped the puppy use his tiny legs to climb his way out of the crate and over to a leaky water spout on the other side of the loading dock, near the dumpster. The puppy stood under the spout looking anxiously from the dripping water to Lassie and back again. He wanted the water very badly, but he couldn't figure out how to get it. He looked up at Lassie and whimpered.

Then Lassie got an idea. The puppy watched as the older dog began searching through an open garbage bag. Lassie used her nose to dig through the mounds of paper, bread, and used straws until she found an old plastic butter tub. It wasn't exactly a water bowl, Lassie thought to herself, but it would certainly do for now.

Lassie clutched the plastic container in her teeth. Ignoring the taste of spoiled butter, she carried the container over to the leaking spout. She placed the butter tub under the drip and watched as it slowly filled with cool, clear water.

The puppy stuck his tiny pink tongue into the plastic container and began to noisily lap up the water.

"Shlurp, shlurp, shlurp, shlurp." The noise was music to Lassie's ears. Lassie looked at the puppy with concern. Why, the poor little fellow obviously hadn't had anything to eat or drink in days! He was licking up the water faster than it was dripping into the container!

Finally, when the puppy had had his fill, Lassie helped him crawl back into his crate. She watched as he used his hind legs to scratch behind his ears. She cocked her head as he grew dizzy moving in circles, chasing his tail. She barked back when he yelped at her and jumped up to play just like any other puppy. Lassie stood patiently while the little fellow jumped on her back and nipped at her legs with his tiny new teeth. The little nips gave the collie great joy instead of great pain. Being with the now-active stray made *Lassie* feel like a puppy again!

After the two dogs had played for a while, the puppy grew tired. He curled up contentedly against the pile of newspapers in his crate and looked up thankfully at Lassie.

Gently, Lassie nuzzled the puppy until he fell asleep, watching as his fuzzy chest moved up and down with each tiny breath.

When the puppy was finally asleep, Lassie looked up at the sky. The sun was starting to set. She'd better be getting home; the McCullochs would be wondering where she had gotten to. The puppy would be alright for the night. He had the rest of the biscuits if he got hungry, and he knew how to get over to his water dish if he got thirsty. Tomorrow, Lassie would bring Will here. Will would know what to do. And if he didn't, his parents certainly would.

With a last look at the sleeping pup, Lassie gave a short sigh and trotted home at a quick, steady pace.

CHAPTER 3

The sun had finally set as Lassie reached home. The three-quarter moon was high in the sky and the street lights on the quiet tree-lined street had just clicked on. The family had left the front door open slightly for Lassie, so the dog let herself in.

The family was already eating, and Lassie stopped in the dining room just long enough to bark "hello" to the McCullochs and Nancy and Neil Shaw, whom Mrs. McCulloch had invited to stay for supper. Then Lassie went straight to the kitchen where her dinner bowl was full and waiting for her.

Lassie had worked up quite an appetite running back and forth to the alleyway. Without ever lifting her head, she gulped down every chunk of meat and lapped up every drop of water in her bowls. Lassie felt happy and secure in the kitchen. The delicious smell of the family's dinner of broiled chicken and mashed potatoes wafted through her nostrils. Even though it had been turned off awhile ago, the heat from the oven was still strong enough to make Lassie feel warm all over. Hearing Will and Megan's laughter float into the kitchen from the dining room made Lassie remember what a loving family she belonged to. A twinge of panic struck in Lassie's stomach as her mind flashed back to the poor lonely puppy in the alley who had no warm, safe home to live in and no happy family to love him.

Well, that would all be taken care of tomorrow, Lassie assured herself. First thing in the morning she would bring Will to see the puppy. Surely the family could find a good home for the poor little guy.

As soon as Lassie was sure there wasn't another morsel of food to eat, she padded out into the family room to spend some time playing with Will, just like she did every night. Maybe tonight they would play fetch, or wrestle on the rug. Better yet, maybe Will would brush Lassie's long, thick coat while they sat quietly, watching TV.

But tonight Will was not alone. He was sitting on the floor with that sad, quiet boy who had been there this afternoon. Lassie couldn't help but be a little disappointed. She really looked forward to her time alone with Will. But the other boy looked so shy and frightened that instead of going to sit by Will, Lassie gently walked closer to the new boy and wagged her tail in a sign of friendship. Instead of smiling at Lassie, Neil sat stiff and uncomfortable, staring, but keeping himself a safe distance from Lassie.

"She won't hurt you, Neil," Will explained gently to the other boy. "Lassie loves kids. Watch." Will turned and faced his beloved collie. "Lassie come . . . Lassie, sit," he commanded.

Obediently, Lassie walked over to her master and sat on her hind legs.

"Good girl," Will complimented Lassie, patting her solidly on the back. He looked lovingly at his dog. Then he turned to Neil. "See how gentle she is?" Will asked him.

But Neil didn't respond to his question. Rather, he sat motionless, staring with new fascination at the beautiful collie that sat before him.

"Lassie's real smart. She can do tricks without me saying anything," Will bragged. "Watch!" Will looked straight at Lassie and raised his hand high in the air.

Lassie's eyes followed the movement of Will's hand. She knew what that meant. Obediently, she stood up on all fours and faced Will. Will smiled and lowered his hand to his side. Lassie sat back down and looked up, watching Will's hand, eagerly waiting for his next unspoken command. Will grinned at her as he turned his hand over so his palm was facing the ceiling. With a happy "woof," Lassie rolled over. Pleased with herself, she looked up at Will, stretching her mouth so that it almost seemed as though she was smiling. Then she looked over to Neil, wagging her tail as if to say, "See, I am a really smart dog!"

Neil was staring at Lassie with interest. Sensing that the boy was starting to relax, Lassie stood up. Instinctively she knew that any fast movement would frighten Neil, so she very slowly inched closer to him. Gently, she sat by his side. This time, Neil didn't move away.

"Give Neil your paw, Lassie," Will said to the collie.

Slowly, Lassie lifted her left front paw and held it out to Neil. Neil looked longingly at the gentle white paw, but try as he might, he could not bring himself to reach out and shake it. Lassie understood. It would take time for this boy to get to know her and be her friend. She dropped her paw and sat very still, letting Neil look her over and become comfortable having her near.

Neil looked from Will to Lassie. Then, very cautiously, he imitated Will by lowering his hand to the ground. Without a thought, Lassie laid down on the floor and looked up happily at Neil.

Getting just a little braver, Neil raised his

hand in the air. Lassie sat up on her hind legs. Finally, Neil mustered up all his courage and put his hand out to Lassie. He wanted to shake her paw. He looked at Lassie hopefully, but the dog didn't move. She wasn't sure what to do. After all, the boy had shied away from her paw before.

"Come on, Lassie," Will said sternly, urging Lassie to shake hands.

Lassie gently placed her paw in Neil's hand and waited. Neil began to shake her paw, gently at first, and then with more enthusiasm.

Neil kept shaking Lassie's paw, staring at her with smiling eyes. He was still holding her paw when his mother came into the room with Mr. and Mrs. McCulloch. Mrs. Shaw stared at her son in surprise. Neil hadn't shaken hands with anyone in his whole life, and here he was playing with Lassie!

"I don't believe it!" she said.

Dee McCulloch smiled at the sight of Neil playing with Lassie. "You can come over and visit Lassie any time you want, Neil," Mrs. McCulloch told him.

Neil didn't look up. He couldn't take his eyes off of his new friend. With his free arm, Neil moved his hand eagerly over her thick gleaming coat. Lassie tipped her head close to Neil's and licked his nose.

Mrs. Shaw gasped. She was sure Neil would

be frightened by Lassie's touch. But instead of pulling away in fear, Neil moved even closer to Lassie and pet her again.

Mrs. Shaw knelt down to talk to her son.

"Neil, honey, it's wonderful you've made a friend," she said calmly. "But we have to go now." She stood up, expecting Neil to follow, but he stayed put, hugging Lassie hard.

"This really is amazing," Mrs. Shaw said to Mrs. McCulloch. "He's always been so afraid of everything." She motioned once again for Neil to get up and get ready to leave, but the boy refused to look at her. He wasn't going anywhere without Lassie.

Will looked at his mother. Then he looked at Neil playing with his collie. A moment of jealousy came over him. Will wanted to tell Neil to get up. He wanted to shout that Lassie was *his* dog, not Neil's, but he just couldn't do it. Will knew that in just a few minutes Lassie had done more for Neil than a lifetime of doctor's visits had achieved. Imagine what Lassie could do for Neil in a whole night! Finally, Will made a tough decision.

With a quivering, unsure voice he said, "Lassie, you go home with Neil tonight."

Neil looked up at Will gratefully. Then he stood up and, leading Lassie by her collar, clumsily made his way to the door.

Mrs. Shaw squeezed Will's shoulders. "Will

. . . thank you," she said, following her son to the door.

Will walked over and opened the door to let them out. Then he bent down and gave Lassie a hug.

"You be a good girl," he whispered in her ear, choking back his tears.

Lassie looked longingly at her master, wanting to stay. She knew that if she left with Neil, it would take her much longer to get Will to help the puppy in the alleyway. Besides, she didn't want to leave her home to go with this stranger! But Will was her master and she had to do as he said. Reluctantly, with her ears dropped and her tail between her legs, she slowly followed Neil out the door.

Will rushed up the stairs and into his room. With a frustrated slam, he closed the door. His parents watched him as he went.

"Tell me this is right," Dee said, looking up at her husband.

"It's only for tonight," Chris answered, trying to assure her.

"Yes, but what about tomorrow?" Dee asked sadly, looking up the stairs toward Will's room.

The McCullochs left Will alone for a while, giving him time to calm down. It was several hours later when Mrs. McCulloch finally knocked softly on his bedroom door.

"Come in," Will muttered.

Will was lying on his bed staring at the ceiling. The only light in the room came from the street lamps outside his window.

"You need another blanket," Dee said, sitting next to Will on the bed. "I'll just throw it over you lightly."

Will looked up at his mother with sad, wet eyes. "This is Lassie's bed," he whispered. "She's never been away from home before."

Dee looked at the bed. Lassie slept with Will every night. The bed did look empty without Lassie. "It does look kind of strange without her. Lassie's one of the family," she said.

"And she's not as much trouble as Megan." Will tried to smile bravely at his feeble joke.

"Well, I don't want to give your sister to the Shaws either."

"No." Will grinned. "But it would be a tough call."

Dee laughed and looked proudly at her son. He was trying so hard to be brave.

"Try and get some sleep," she suggested. "It will be all right. Lassie is our dog."

"I know, but it's not all right. One thing really worries me."

"What's that?"

"What if Neil needs Lassie more than I do?"

Mrs. McCulloch looked at Will. She had no answers for him. All she could do was reach over, stroke his unruly brown hair, and give him a long, tight hug.

Meanwhile, Lassie was wide awake in Neil's room. She felt uncomfortable lying in this strange bed with a strange boy. Neil's arm was draped securely across her broad back. It was as if he couldn't bear to let go of her, even in his sleep. Lassie looked mournfully at the open window across the room and whimpered quietly. It would be so easy to free herself from Neil's grasp, jump out the window, and run home to sleep in Will's bed. But Will had commanded her to go with Neil. He had told her to be a good girl. Lassie sighed. Oh well, she thought. It was just for one night. Tomorrow she would go home. Tomorrow she would be with Will. Tomorrow she would get help for the dog she had befriended in the alleyway. Tomorrow everything would be alright.

With tomorrow on her mind, Lassie finally settled in and fell asleep.

CHAPTER 4

The sun was just coming up when Lassie heard the loud roar of the garbage truck driving down the street, stopping at each house. The sound of the truck's mighty engine, the shouts of the men as they lifted the heavy cans, and the slamming of the metal as they put the empty cans down again, startled the collie awake. She opened her eyes slowly, blinking them once or twice. She tossed her head, trying to shake away the sleep. Then, she became confused. She sniffed the air. There was no familiar scent of bacon frying in the kitchen. Her sensitive ears picked up the sound of nervous, uneven childish breathing, instead of Will's peaceful little snore. For a second, Lassie was afraid. She'd forgotten she was not at home and she wasn't sure where she was. But when she looked over and saw Neil sleeping beside her, the events of the night before came back to her.

Roar . . . slam . . . roar. The garbage truck was moving on to the next house. Garbage! Lassie's body stiffened suddenly. The alleyway! It wouldn't be long before the garbage truck reached the crates in the back of the alleyway! The puppy was there all alone. What if the garbage collectors dumped the crates into their truck and drove off! She would never find the puppy!

Lassie knew you couldn't trust all humans to be kind to dogs. Who knew if these garbage men were the types who might hurt a poor defenseless puppy! She had to get out of this place and rescue the stray.

Neil's arm was clinging tightly around Lassie's body. At first, she stirred slightly, moving her body very gently, trying to free herself from Neil's grip. The boy held tight. Lassie weighed her options carefully. If she struggled hard enough to free herself, she would surely wake the boy. If she stayed put, something awful might happen to the stray pup. She had no choice! This was no time for consideration. Neil would just have to lose some sleep! She had to get moving and beat that truck to the alleyway. Time was running out! With a sudden push of her strong legs, Lassie stood up on the bed, forcing Neil's arm to jerk off of her. Without wasting a second, Lassie dashed across the little room and with a single flying leap, jumped right out of the bedroom window.

Luckily, Neil's bedroom was on the first floor of the house, so the drop from his bedroom window wasn't too far. Still, when Lassie landed on the soft flower beds beneath his window, she felt a shock of pressure rush through her paws and up her legs to her back. There was no time to check herself for injuries, though. She had an important job to do! In a split second, Lassie started moving like a golden brown and white meteor, shooting down the streets of Glen Ridge at what seemed like the speed of light, to the stray's hideout.

Back in the alleyway, the lonely puppy was doing a little moving of his own. He had no way of knowing that Lassie was on her way with help. All he knew was that his stomach was grumbling. He had finished eating the biscuits Lassie had brought him last night. They had made a great midnight snack. But now it was morning, and he was ready for breakfast. The heat of the rising sun made the scent of the scraps of old meat, stale rolls, and rotted tomatoes from the workers' left-over garbage rise out from inside the dumpster that stood across the loading dock from the pile of crates. The scent of the food excited the puppy. He could almost taste it. His mouth started to drool and his stomach grumbled. He got up on his hind legs and jumped for joy, wagging his scraggly tail.

Then, with a happy "awruff" he quickly climbed his way out of the crate and onto the loading dock.

The puppy could feel the rickety old loading dock shake under him as walked over to his water dish. His nails made a *click-click-clicking* sound against the metal. After a few drinks of water, the puppy was ready to continue his trek to the food in the dumpster.

When he finally reached the end of the loading dock, he noticed he was still a few feet from the dumpster. The only thing connecting the loading dock to the garbage was a splintery old plank that formed a wobbly, rotting bridge by resting on one side along the loading dock and leaning across the opening of the dumpster on the other.

Even though the pup had been through a great deal of suffering, he was, after all, a baby. Like any baby of any species, the puppy didn't think about danger. So, without stopping to test the sturdiness of the "bridge," he wandered full force onto the plank.

As the little fellow crossed the plank, he thought eagerly of the food that awaited him. The smells delighted his twitchy little black pug nose. He was almost there. If he could just make it across that plank to the dumpster, the banquet that awaited was his.

A few more steps and the plank teetered back and forth. The puppy stopped moving for a second, waiting for the plank to regain its delicate balance. When the plank stopped shaking, the puppy moved on, stepping just a little bit slower this time. His feet wobbled only slightly as he walked along the splintery plank. Finally the stray reached the dumpster. He stood on the edge of the shaky wooden plank and craned his neck into the dumpster. There he spied a scrap of fatty roast beef. Yummy! But before he could reach for it, his weight threw the plank off balance. It slipped off its perch between the dock and the garbage bin and slid to the ground, throwing the frightened puppy into the dumpster.

It was dark in the dumpster. The small puppy was petrified. He couldn't see anything, and the smell of rancid food was making him ill. He certainly didn't feel much like eating the food now. He was too frightened. And he didn't like the feel of wet, moldy vegetables rubbing and sticking against his fur either. Frantically, the puppy jumped up, trying to leap out of the dumpster. But the walls were too high, and his legs were too short to make that kind of leap. The puppy started to panic. He jumped up again and again, throwing his tiny body against the side of the dumpster. The walls let out a small thud. The stray barked feverishly, hoping someone would hear him.

Finally, Lassie arrived at the alley. Immediately, she went to the pile of crates and looked in the very bottom one for the puppy. The collie's mighty heart skipped a beat. The puppy was gone! Had something happened to him? If he had been injured, Lassie knew she would never forgive herself.

"Yip! Yip! Yip!" the puppy barked.

Lassie breathed a heavy sigh of relief. She would know that bark anywhere! The puppy was somewhere in the alley. Lassie looked around. But where?

"Roof! Roof!" Lassie called to the stray.

"Yip!"

Lassie turned. The sound was coming from the dumpster next to the loading dock. The puppy was in the dumpster! But how did he get in there, she wondered? Then Lassie spotted the fallen plank. Turning her nose up, she smelled the food in the pile of garbage in the dumpster. So *that* was what had happened.

"Ruff! Ruff! Ruff!" Lassie shouted. It was her way of telling the puppy not to panic. She would get him out of there. Carefully taking the splintery plank in her mouth, Lassie leaped onto the old rusty loading dock on the other side of the garbage bin. Very slowly, she slid the plank into the dumpster, leaning it on the edge of the loading dock. As she used her front paws to hold the plank steady, Lassie barked an order to the puppy. She wanted him to climb up the plank.

The puppy placed his front paws on the plank and tried to make his way up to the top where Lassie stood, waiting. But the plank was at too steep an angle, and as he tried to move his back paws up the plank, the puppy went sliding right back into the garbage.

"Ruff! Ruff!" Lassie ordered the puppy to try again.

Shaking himself off, the stray stood and tried again, but his legs weren't able to carry him up such a steep incline. Once again, he went sliding down into the darkness of the dumpster.

Lassie looked around. There had to be something in the alley that she could use to get the puppy out of the garbage dumpster. As she searched the alley, she kept her pointy ears pricked up high. Her keen sense of hearing was picking up the distant hum of a powerful motor. The garbage truck! It would be here soon!

Lassie started to panic. If she didn't think of something right away, the tiny puppy would be thrown into the garbage truck and crushed in its mighty jaws!

CHAPTER 5

Sometimes help comes from the most unexpected sources. As Lassie stood helplessly in the alley, barking with all her might, she had no way of knowing that by waking Neil, she had sent for help.

When Lassie had left Neil's room, she had woken the boy. Neil, half asleep, had groped listlessly for his new friend. But of course, Lassie was long gone. Sitting up in bed, Neil had spotted the open window. It had taken Neil only a few seconds to figure out that Lassie had woken up and jumped out the window.

Lassie would never have expected the quiet child to follow her, but that was because she hadn't realized how much Neil valued his newfound friendship with the kind and gentle collie. When he had discovered her missing, Neil had put on his slippers, followed her lead, and jumped out the window—without even changing out of his thin cotton pajamas!

Now, as he wandered the empty streets in the glow of the early morning light, Neil was scared. He had never been alone in the town before, and he had no idea where he was. The only thing the boy knew was that he had to find Lassie. Unfortunately, he hadn't a clue as to where the collie could be.

Not only didn't he know where *Lassie* was, Neil didn't even know where *he* was at this moment. He was lost! Tears smarted in his eyes, and he broke into a cold sweat. Standing in one place, Neil shivered as he felt the cool morning wind blowing through his damp cotton pajamas.

By some unexplainable miracle, Neil had wandered by the puppy's alley hideout. As he stood motionless, looking teary-eyed at the empty parked cars and the closed, dark warehouses, Neil heard a thunderously trumpeting series of barks coming from his left. "Ruff! Ruff! Ruff! Ruff!"

Lassie! Neil heaved a sigh of relief! He found Lassie! Everything would be okay now!

Joyously, Neil went running into the alley. For the first time in his life, Neil was not afraid of a new place. He bounded over the garbage to Lassie and grabbed her around her thick, bearded neck. But Lassie shook him off with all her might and gave a gruff snort. This was no time for a happy reunion.

Immediately, the brave collie got down to business. She turned and faced the dumpster. "Ruff! Ruff! Ruff!" Barking as furiously as she could, Lassie tried to tell Neil about the trapped puppy. But Neil didn't understand Lassie's desperate cries. Will would have gotten the message, but Neil didn't know Lassie the way Will did. Neil hadn't grown up understanding Lassie's special, almost human language the way Will had.

Lassie's forehead creased as her mind raced in an attempt to think of another plan to get Neil into that dumpster. Sensing that Neil would follow her anywhere, Lassie walked onto the rusty loading dock and over to the dumpster. Neil did indeed follow, ignoring the rotted food and corroded paper that had fallen around the great garbage bin. Lassie stopped by the dumpster and stood silently.

"Yip! Yip! Yip!" the puppy wailed from inside his dark prison. Neil heard the muffled cries of panic coming from the gray metal dumpster. He looked from Lassie to the dumpster and back again. Lassie studied his face and began to relax. He understood! The boy understood!

Lassie's relief was short-lived. Neil may have understood, but he didn't make a move toward the dumpster. The dumpster was so big and smelly that Neil was too afraid to reach in. He stood motionless, his big eyes pleading with Lassie not to ask this of him.

But Lassie was persistent. She barked angrily at Neil, and gestured at the dumpster with her mighty head. She felt sorry for the boy, but she was getting a bit tired of his cowardice!

Neil loved Lassie more than he had ever loved anyone—other than his mother. He would do anything to please her! If this was what she wanted, he thought to himself, then he would have to climb into the dark, ominous garbage bin and get the imprisoned dog. He took one last, loving look at Lassie. Then, inhaling a deep breath, Neil leaned over the top of the dumpster and pushed himself in. The drop was deeper than he expected, and he lost his breath for a second as he landed with a dull, heavy thud on a pile of rotted food and discarded Styrofoam cups.

Inside the dumpster, the little puppy looked at his potential saviour with huge, frightened eyes. He barked so quietly it was practically a whisper. "Friend or foe?" he seemed to be asking Neil.

Somehow, Neil understood. He answered the puppy by scooping him up in his arms and giving the puppy a warm, loving squeeze. The pup responded by snuggling quietly against Neil's chest and looking up at his face. Instinctively, the stray knew he could trust this large two-legged creature with eyes as sad and lonely as his own.

Holding the puppy tight, Neil tried to climb up and out of the dumpster and onto the loading dock. But the dumpster was too deep for him. There was nothing for him to hold on to. Without letting go of the poor puppy, Neil quickly gathered the largest pieces of trash together to form a mountain of garbage. He tried to pile up enough food and cups to build a step stool, but the pile of old lunch meat, packing crates and vegetables crumbled under his weight. Neil shuddered. There wasn't anything he could do. There was nothing to climb up on; no way out!

Then, as if the boy weren't frightened enough, he suddenly heard the roar of an oncoming garbage pickup truck. The sound grew stronger as the truck moved into the alley! Neil cowered in fear against the side of the dumpster, clutching the puppy for dear life.

The mighty pickup stopped at the edge of the alley. The driver of the truck flicked a switch and a giant fork with two huge, sharp fangs dove into a dumpster and tilted it over. Mountains of smelly, filthy trash spilled out of the dumpster and into the huge vat in the back of the truck. Then, when the dumpster was empty, the truck operator flicked another switch, and the giant fork set the dumpster right side up again. Then the truck moved on to the next dumpster—the one where Neil and the stray were trapped!

Lassie sprang into action!

In desperation, she threw all of her eighty pounds against the slow-moving truck, barking so hard she thought she might burst. The truck squealed to a halt. The driver of the pickup jumped down from his seat and walked in front of the truck to look at the dog. He was sure she had been hurt.

But Lassie wasn't hurt, the truck had been moving far too slowly to harm her. Lassie barked furiously. She was anxious to stop the man from lowering the deadly fork onto her friends. Jumping up and down, Lassie barked ferociously at the man. She jumped so high and with such force that at times she was looking this full grown man straight in the eye. He flinched as he felt her hot breath on his face. He jumped back in surprise when he saw her sharp, milky-white teeth glowing from her dark cavernous mouth.

"Move along now, get out of my way!" the dumptruck operator shouted at the wild, jumping collie. He moved his hand to shoo her from the dumpster, but Lassie stood her ground, jumping wildly, and barking her most ferocious bark.

"I said out of my way you crazy dog!" the driver shouted at Lassie again. But the driver moved a little farther from the dumpster. He couldn't be sure, but he thought this wild, wolflike collie was staring at his throat with the look of a maniacal killer! Even if he was just imagining it, the driver wasn't taking any chances with what he was sure was a mad dog.

Lassie didn't move any closer toward the man, but she did keep on shouting her long, piercing, pressing barks. Maybe she could force this human to get in his truck and leave. Or maybe she could attract the attention of someone who understood what she was trying to say!

"Ruff! Ruff! Ruff!" she cried, louder and louder. "Ruff! Ruff! Ruff!"

CHAPTER 6

"All I know is Neil is gone, Lassie is gone, and I don't know when they left," Nancy Shaw was saying hopelessly to Dee and Chris McCulloch as they drove through the empty streets of Glen Ridge in search of Neil and Lassie.

At about 7:00 that morning, Mrs. Shaw had gotten up and gone to Neil's room to ask him if he was ready for breakfast. She had knocked twice on the thin wooden door. Nobody had answered. Thinking Neil and Lassie were sleeping late, she had walked in the room to wake the sleepyheads. But instead of a sleeping boy and a collie, Nancy Shaw had found rumpled sheets on the bed, a blanket on the floor, and an open window. In a panic, she had called the McCullochs and asked them to help her find her son.

Chris, Dee, and Will were already awake. But

Megan was not. And she was not at all pleased when Dee came bursting into her room, rousing her from her sleep. Megan was in the middle of an especially fantastic dream about winning the Pulitzer prize for best news photograph when her mother shook her and ordered her to get dressed and come look for Lassie and Neil.

Fifteen minutes later, the McCullochs picked up Nancy Shaw in their gleaming black 4X4. Now they were driving through the streets of Glen Ridge on their search for a missing boy and a dog. The town seemed strangely empty at such an early hour.

"We'll find them," Dee McCulloch said comfortingly to Nancy Shaw.

"We'll cover every street between our house and yours," Chris guaranteed, keeping his eyes peeled on the road ahead. He stopped briefly at an intersection and looked out his rearview mirror for some sign of either Neil or Lassie.

"Someone must have seen them," Megan said hopefully, just barely covering a tired yawn.

Dee tried to agree with her daughter's hopeful outlook, but staring out at the empty streets of Glen Ridge, she doubted very much that anyone was around to spot a dog and a boy in his pajamas walking the streets. So far she herself had only seen two drivers and a couple of garbagemen on the streets.

Nancy Shaw choked back her tears. "Neil's never done anything like this before!" she explained.

"Don't worry Mrs. Shaw," Will said proudly. "Lassie's with him!"

But Nancy Shaw didn't know Lassie like Will did. She took little comfort in the knowledge that her troubled son was wandering the streets at dawn with only a dog for protection. And somehow, Nancy Shaw was sure the collie was responsible for Neil's disappearance!

Glen Ridge was as quiet as a ghost town. A person could hear a pin drop. Or in this case, a dog bark. Good thing, too. For as Chris stopped at a red light, Will heard a distant "ruff!"

"Dad! Wait! Stop!" Will shouted at his father. He was so excited he nearly jumped out of his seat.

"What is it?" Mrs. Shaw asked.

"Lassie!" Will smiled.

"You see her?" Dee McCulloch asked. She looked around the street. There was no sign of the collie.

"No, I hear her! She's in that alley we just passed."

Nancy Shaw looked doubtfully at Will. How could he tell that it was Lassie barking?

"There must be hundreds of stray dogs running around this part of town, Will," Nancy Shaw exclaimed. "How do you know that bark was Lassie's?"

Will knew Lassie's sharp, hearty bark like he knew his own voice. "It's Lassie, Mrs. Shaw," he said. "Trust me." He was absolutely sure he heard Lassie and no other dog.

Chris was sure of it, too. He hadn't heard a bark, but if Will said he heard Lassie in the alley, then they would go to the alley. With one turn of his strong arms, Chris McCulloch turned the steering wheel, and with a loud screech, the 4X4 made a U-turn and drove back to the opening of the alleyway.

Will barely waited for the 4X4 to stop before he jumped out the door and into the alley. "There she is," he shouted to his parents and his sister. "It's Lassie!" He motioned for them to follow him.

Will ran at top speed toward his collie. When he reached her, he hugged her tight around the thick mat of gold and white hair that protected her neck, and kissed her smooth forehead.

Lassie jumped up and licked Will's face. She nearly knocked him over with her excitement. Was she glad to see him!

Nancy Shaw smiled briefly at the happy scene, but her grin turned almost instantly to a worried frown.

"Where's Neil?" she asked Dee.

Dee smiled reassuringly at her concerned

friend. "I have a feeling Lassie knows," she said, nodding toward the collie. Lassie had left Will's side and was already barking her loud, trumpeting bark in the direction of the dumpster.

"Is that your crazy dog?" the dumpster pickup operator asked Chris McCulloch gruffly. He was obviously relieved to see the dog's owners had arrived. Their presence had given him courage, and he spoke angrily at Chris.

"Get her out of here! I've got work to do! She's been barking like a mad dog all morning!"

The man made a move toward the dumpster. He was sure the dog wouldn't act crazy in front of her master. But Lassie barked louder than ever and charged up onto the loading dock. The dumpster operator jumped back in surprise. He glowered at Chris.

"Wait a minute, Mister," Will pleaded with the pickup operator. The man said nothing, but he didn't make a move toward his truck.

Will and his father followed Lassie onto the rusty old dock. When they finally reached the rusted bin, Will craned his neck to look into the dumpster. There, among the piles of spoiled food, paper, and plastic he saw Neil and a puppy huddled in a corner. A big smile flashed on Will's face. He looked over to his mother and flashed a V-for-victory sign.

"It's Neil," he called over to the three women standing below. "He's in the dumpster!"

Nancy Shaw ran up the stairs and onto the loading dock. "Where is he?" she screamed. "Where is my son?"

The truck operator looked shaken.

"My goodness! A kid's in there?" He looked sheepishly at Dee and Megan. "I would have killed him!"

Will hugged his heroic collie tight. "If it hadn't been for you," he said proudly to Lassie. His dog was a hero! Lassie looked up and licked Will's face.

"That dog knew?" the pickup operator asked in disbelief.

Will nodded quickly. Then he went back to hugging and petting Lassie.

Chris McCulloch reached down deep into the dumpster and, using all of his strength, lifted Neil out of the garbage heap. As he was being lifted up, Neil held tight to the frightened, abandoned puppy he had tried so hard to rescue. When they reached the dock, Chris set the boy down and wiped the sweat from his own brow.

Everyone smiled at Neil with relief. He looked dirty, and scared. His pajamas were wet with perspiration, and he smelled just awful, but he wasn't hurt. The stray was doing just fine, too. The puppy blinked its eyes a few times as the bright sunlight hit him, but he made no move to scurry from his comfortable seat in Neil's arms.

Nancy Shaw ran over to Neil and hugged him harder than she ever had before. "You're alright; you're alright," she said over and over again as the tears of joy and relief rolled shamelessly down her cheeks.

"I'll say he's alright," Chris McCulloch exclaimed. Then he gently took the stray from Neil's arms. "He saved this little dog's life."

"Poor little guy's been abandoned," Dee McCulloch said softly as she scratched the puppy's matted head.

"Yeah," Will added sadly.

Neil looked down at Lassie. He had done all this for her. She had needed him. Then he looked at the puppy. He had needed Neil, too.

"He's all alone," Megan said gently to Neil as she pointed to the stray.

"You saved him. You're responsible for him," Will told Neil.

Neil stood, staring at the puppy in Chris's arms. Lassie didn't need him anymore. She had Will. But this puppy needed him as much as he needed the puppy! Ever so slowly, Neil walked over to Chris and put his cheek next to the scraggly face of the puppy. The puppy stuck out his tiny pink tongue and licked Neil right on the nose. Neil put out his hands with a new steadiness, and took the puppy in his arms. He hugged him tightly. Then he looked up cheerfully at his mother.

"Mine," he said simply.

It was the first word Neil had said in years. This sweet little puppy had begun to break down the walls of silence Neil had built up! Nancy Shaw looked at her son through wet eyes. "Yes, Neil," she said. "He's yours." Then she hugged her son and his dog.

Chris McCulloch put his arm around Will. "A boy needs a dog," he said.

Dee looked from Lassie to the puppy. "A dog needs a boy," she added.

Lassie jumped up and licked Will on the cheek. She couldn't have agreed more!

BURIED TREASURE

A Novel by Nancy E. Krulik
Based on the Al Burton Production
Adapted from the episode "POT HUNTERS"
Written by Cathryn Michon & Eric Vennerbeck

CHAPTER
1

"Ruff! Ruff! Ruff!"

Lassie barked with joy and reckless enthusiasm as she ran playfully across the muddy field. This was just the kind of afternoon the beautiful, purebred collie loved. Nothing made her happier than playing in an open field with Will and Megan McCulloch. Lassie had lived with the McCulloch family since she was just a pup, and she had grown up with fourteen-year-old Megan and ten-year-old Will. The two kids meant more to her than anything else in the world.

Right at this moment, Lassie was completely content. Feeling the northern California sun beat down on her thick, downy, white and golden coat and hearing the laughter of the two children she loved most made Lassie feel as carefree as a puppy.

Today, Lassie was playing a game of chase-the-airplane with Will. Will was flying his brand-new remote-controlled World War I model biplane in the air. Will loved model airplanes. He would spend hours in his room sitting patiently at his desk, putting hundreds of delicate plastic and metal pieces together until they formed an exact replica of a famous airplane. Will was fascinated by airplanes and famous pilots. He even resembled a pilot today in his dark, wire-framed aviator sunglasses.

As Will moved the joystick up and down on its pad, the plane did flips and loops in the air. Lassie tried her best to catch it. As the plane flew overhead, buzzing like a swarm of attacking bees, Lassie watched like a wolf tracking its prey. She kept her pointy ears straight up, listening to the hum of the plane's engine. Her slanted collie eyes never left the shiny flying toy for a second. As she ran, Lassie held her regal head high in the air and wagged her thick, tawny tail fast and joyously. Her mouth was pulled back so far that it looked almost as though she were grinning a big, toothsome grin.

As the remote-control toy airplane flew over her head, Lassie jumped high in the air and opened her mouth wide. She was trying desperately to catch the plane. In her dog mind, Lassie thought she and Will, the boy who was her master, were playing their old game of fetch. But to Lassie's surprise, as soon as she jumped up to reach the model airplane, the plane moved even higher, as though the toy had a mind of its own.

Of course, the plane didn't have a mind at all. It shifted its course only because Will had moved the joystick that controlled it. But Lassie couldn't know this. Confused, the mighty collie stood on her powerful hind legs and jumped around in a circle, following the plane with her eyes as it flew off over a hill.

Will watched his dog dance in confusion. It was a very funny sight—a purebred, strong and mighty collie performing a wild ballet in the middle of a field. He laughed so hard that he lost control of the joystick. The plane's engine sputtered and the toy tailspinned its way to a crash landing in the mud. Lassie's sensitive ears picked up the sound of the crash. Immediately she ran to the plane.

"Aarghh! There goes my plane," Will shouted angrily to no one in particular.

"Aarghh! There goes my picture!" Megan shouted angrily at her younger brother. She had been taking photographs of the flying plane in the hopes of having them published in her high school newspaper. Meg was an avid photographer. She never went anywhere without her camera. Someday she wanted to be a professional photographer.

Nothing would make Meg happier than getting paid for one of her photographs.

But Will wasn't thinking about Meg's pictures. "I hope I didn't ruin my plane," he said as he high-tailed it over to where his new toy had plummeted to the ground. After all, the toy had cost him a month's allowance to buy and had taken two weeks of hard work to put together. Meg followed close behind Will as he headed toward the crashed plane.

As they ran, Meg and Will passed by their father, Chris McCulloch, and his younger brother, the kids' Uncle Steve. Chris McCulloch owned one of the most successful construction companies in Glen Ridge, California. The field that Will was using for an airport was really the construction site for a new warehouse Chris's firm was building. Chris had brought his brother along for company while he made some notes on the layout of the field. The kids had tagged along, too, so they could play in the open field while their dad worked.

"The Red Baron crashed!" Will shouted over to his father, pointing to the fallen plane.

"Well I'm glad it was an enemy plane, and not one of ours," Chris joked back to his son. The Red Baron was the nickname of a German fighter pilot during World War I.

Will bent down to pick up the pieces of his crashed plane.

"Wait, don't move it!" Megan warned him. Quickly she got her camera out of its case, adjusted the lens, and started clicking away.

Will looked at her as though she were crazy. Why would anyone want to take a picture of a broken toy airplane? "There's nothing to move. It's a total disaster," he said. "The struts are all broken and the prop is all twisted."

Megan didn't even look up. She just moved slowly around the plane, photographing the wreckage from different angles.

"It's perfect," she mumbled.

Will was getting annoyed. Sometimes his sister could really be strange. He sighed as he bent down and picked up the pieces of his plane.

"Hey!" Megan argued, looking fiercely at her brother. She wasn't through with it yet.

Will looked behind him. There was Lassie, digging in the ground. She had created quite a deep hole. The soft mud had almost completely covered her white paws.

"What's this, girl?" he asked, walking over to see what was keeping Lassie so fascinated.

Lassie's digging had brought a piece of fiery red clay to the surface.

Will bent down and brushed the dirt away from the clay. Lassie moved out of the way to let Will get closer to the dull object. Gently, Will dug under the piece of clay and pulled up the jagged remains of an old handmade clay pot.

Will held the treasure carefully in his two hands and stared at it. The red piece of pottery was covered with intricately carved designs of triangles, circles, and dots. Bits of color still marked the pattern, but time had worn most of the original paint away.

"Hey, Dad, look at this," Will shouted over to his father. Chris and Steve stopped what they were doing and came over to the hill to take a look.

"It looks old," Megan said as Will gingerly handed the small piece of art to his father.

"Mmmm . . . very old," Chris answered, turning the small piece of pottery around in his hands as he studied the designs more carefully. "These look like Indian designs."

Will looked at his uncle. "Hey, Uncle Steve, look what we found," he said proudly.

Steve McCulloch was a freelance news reporter. Like most reporters, he knew something about a lot of subjects. It almost seemed that no matter what the kids said or did, Uncle Steve had written an article that could relate to the topic at hand.

"I did an article on the local Indians one time," he said. Megan and Will looked at each other with stifled grins. They knew their uncle would have a story. "These are Chumash Indian symbols." He pointed to a large round circle. "That's Awha'y—the moon." He pointed to another symbol. "That's Hutash—the earth goddess . . ."

"It's real!" Will interrupted excitedly.

"Could be four hundred years old," Uncle Steve told him.

Will had an exciting idea. "This could have been an Indian burial ground!" he said.

Megan's blue eyes shone with the same excitement. "We've found buried treasure!"

"We'll all be rich!" Will shouted.

Megan was so excited she nearly pounced on Lassie. "Lassie, you're a genius!" she laughed as she hugged her around her broad shaggy back. Lassie barked with glee and wagged her tail. She wasn't sure what she had done that was so wonderful, but making Megan and Will happy was what Lassie lived for. If they were happy, she was happy!

Megan snapped to attention. "If there's one, there could be more," she cried. "Let's look!" She and Will bent down and started to dig feverishly into the ground.

"Let's not," their father said solemnly, staring off at the field. "We've taken enough from the Indians already. And there are laws. Any digging on a tribal site is done under Indian supervision.

And Uncle Steve didn't say this was a burial site. Maybe what was here was just a . . . village."

"A huge village," Megan said, her voice jumping up with excitement.

"The hugest!" Will countered.

"There could be a lot of stuff here," Megan said to her brother.

The kids' enthusiasm was catching. "You've just uncovered a great story," Uncle Steve chimed in. "And we've got a hook for it. The discovery was made by . . ."

"A kid!" Will broke in. "Young Indiana McCulloch." Will struck an Indiana Jones–like pose by the hole.

"Woof! Woof! Woof!" Lassie barked, pushing Will out of the way.

"That's right, Lassie," Chris said smiling. "You found it first!" He pointed at Lassie. "Ladies and gentlemen . . . I give you Lassie, the world's greatest canine archaeologist!" he joked.

"Hey, if Lassie's famous, I'll be famous," Will said smiling.

His family looked at him curiously.

"Somebody has to be her spokesperson," he explained.

Lassie barked angrily at the boy. Everyone laughed.

"Well, maybe not . . ." Will continued.

Uncle Steve looked closer at the ancient pot.

"And I know just the photographer to cover the story," he said.

Megan's interest grew stronger. "Who's that?" she asked hopefully.

As an answer, Uncle Steve put his arm around her shoulder. Megan looked up at him with grateful eyes. "Me?" she asked in amazement.

"It's a natural." Her uncle smiled down at her. "A lot of magazines would snap it up. We could get three . . . four thousand dollars . . . easy!"

Three or four thousand dollars! Megan couldn't believe it. " 'We?' " she repeated. "You and me?"

"We'll split it right down the middle."

Megan did some quick division in her head. Four thousand divided by two. "Two thousand dollars," she muttered.

"Megan, it's very exciting," her father said slowly. "But I don't want you to get your hopes up too high."

"You're right," Megan said dreamily. "Okay . . . maybe a thousand dollars." She turned to her brother. "You can be famous," she joked. "I'll be famous and rich! I'll be . . ."

"Very irritating!" Will snapped back.

CHAPTER 2

"I mean it! She could have her pictures published," Steve McCulloch said earnestly to his brother, Chris, and his sister-in-law, Dee. It was late in the afternoon, and Chris and Steve were sitting on the family room couch, arguing over Steve's new partnership with his niece.

Dee didn't even look up. She was sitting on the chair by her desk in the McCulloch's family room, studying the ancient clay pot her kids had brought home. Her kids had practically exploded into the house earlier in the afternoon shouting something about Lassie, Indians, and buried treasure. Dee owned her own personnel business and she had been hard at work at home when the kids and Lassie found the clay pot. Now, she was too busy just trying to sort things out to get involved in the argument between her husband and her brother-in-law. Besides, this was something the brothers had to work out between themselves.

"I just don't want Megan to be disappointed," Chris tried to explain to his brother. He was afraid the photographs would never get sold to any magazine. Chris was not nearly as optimistic about the sale as his younger brother was.

"She will be disappointed . . . if you don't let her try," Steve remarked angrily to his brother.

That kind of logic was hard to argue with. "Well . . ." Chris considered. "Okay, if we're going to make a story, let's do it. First let's call the experts and find out what's really there."

At that point in the conversation Dee popped her head up and announced excitedly, "Grace Dickenson!"

Chris and Steve laughed at her outburst, then stared at her curiously.

"Who?" Chris asked.

"From college," Dee explained as she got up and moved toward the phone that sat on her desk. "Grace was my 'big sister' in my college sorority. She was the one who taught me all the rules, helped me make friends. She was my idol. Last I heard she was an archaeology professor at Freemont University. I'll just give her a call and see if she can help. I'll try information and get the number of the school." Dee was very excited—both about the pot the kids and Lassie had found, and even more so, about the possibility that the pot would give her the opportunity of seeing the woman she had idolized all through college! Dee's fingers practically flew over the push buttons on the phone as she dialed the number of the Freemont University switchboard.

Steve and Chris sat patiently as Dee dialed the number, went through the university operator, and caught up with Grace Dickenson in her office.

Upon hearing her old chum's familiar voice on the phone, Dee had to choke back a desire to spend the phone call reminiscing about the good old days in their college sorority. (After all, she was calling for business reasons, Dee reminded herself.) Quickly, Dee explained about the warehouse development site, and the ancient clay pot Lassie had dug up there. Grace listened attentively on the other end, taking notes at a feverish pace. When Dee finished giving her the details of the time, the exact location of the site and the size and description of the clay pot, Grace agreed to come to the McCullochs's to examine Lassie's find.

"It's terrific we're getting together again, Dee Dee," Grace said using Dee's college nickname. "Imagine, all these years and it took an Indian relic to bring us together again!" Then she paused and whispered so quietly into the phone that Dee had to strain to hear her. "Oh and please, Dee Dee, don't mention this to anyone."

"Okay, Grace, sure," Dee agreed, with a question in her voice. "See you tomorrow then."

With a quizzical look on her face, Dee hung up the phone and turned back to the anxious Steve and Chris.

"Well?" Chris asked his wife.

"She'll be here tomorrow afternoon," Dee said, absentmindedly, her thoughts still on Grace's last comment. "It's going to be fun seeing her again. One thing concerns me though."

"You think you've put on weight since you saw her last," Chris teased his wife.

Dee grinned back at him. "No, have I?" she asked suddenly, glancing in a mirror.

"No!" Chris assured her, giving her a playful tap.

"Ahem . . . Then what is bothering you about the phone call, Dee?" Steve interrupted.

Dee turned to him. "It's just that Grace said the oddest thing just now," Dee explained. "She said 'Don't mention this to anyone.' "

Megan was just walking through the back door of the house and into the family room and she heard the tail end of the conversation between her parents and Uncle Steve.

"Don't mention what to anyone?" she asked her mother as she flopped down on the comfortable couch and put her sandaled feet up on the coffee table.

"Your mother asked a friend of hers who is an archaeologist to take a look at the clay pot Lassie found today," Chris explained to his daughter. Megan looked excited at the prospect. A real archaeologist! Right here in their house. And the archaeologist was a friend of her mother's! Her mother sure was full of surprises!

"Maybe she's afraid of pothunters," Steve thought out loud.

Megan giggled. "Pot holders?" she asked. Sometimes Uncle Steve could be so weird!

"Pothunters." Steve corrected his niece with an unexpected tone of seriousness in his voice. "Looters, grave robbers. Any one of these pots could be worth thousands," he explained as he picked up the Indian pot.

"Oooh! Just like *Raiders of the Lost Ark*!" Megan squealed. Megan loved the Indiana Jones series of fast-action movies.

"Exactly," Uncle Steve said seriously. "They'll clean the place out, and you can't prove a thing! After all, nobody knows what is actually buried there."

Megan's eyes grew dreamy. She was imagining herself in the middle of an exciting Indiana Jones–like mystery-adventure story. "You could catch them in the act . . ." she began.

Uncle Steve cut her story short. "Listen, Nancy Drew," he said, taking Megan by the shoulders. "These aren't nice characters combing the beach for small change. They're criminals."

Megan sat back on the couch and let the warning set in. Then, without saying another word, she walked quietly out of the family room and upstairs to her room.

Dee and Chris stared at each other. Looters! Criminals! What had they gotten themselves into?

Steve noted the panic on his brother's and sister-in-law's faces. "I think I set her straight," Steve told them. "She won't go back there, now."

But Uncle Steve didn't know his niece as well as he thought. At that very moment, Megan and Will were with Lassie sitting on Will's bed discussing their next trip back to the field.

"I have to get better shots for the article," Meg was saying.

"We'd better do it before the archaeologists dig the whole place up," Will agreed.

Megan sat silently for a second. She was thinking about what Uncle Steve had said about the pothunters. It had sounded pretty dangerous.

"I know, except . . ." she began.

"Except what?" Will asked.

Megan sighed. She really wanted those photographs. "Oh, nothing. Just something Uncle Steve said. Maybe we shouldn't tell anyone. Scientists, parents, you never know what they're going to say."

Will agreed. "Right! We'll get all your shots tomorrow afternoon. Lassie and I will meet you there right after school . . . Three-thirty."

Megan smiled. On the outside, she looked confident—for Will's sake. But inside, the things Uncle Steve had told her made her afraid.

What the McCullochs didn't know was that their worst fears were already coming true. The pothunters had indeed found out about the Indian relics and were already making plans to clean the ancient burial site out. And at this very moment, the brains behind the ring of thieves was organizing everything. The most upsetting part was that the dishonest leader was none other than Grace Dickenson—Dee's old friend!

As soon as she had hung up with Dee, Grace had shut the door to her office and dialed her fellow pothunters. Now she was hard at work, planning the job with them on the phone.

"Yep, it looks like we finally hit it!" she said to the man on the other end of the phone. "Right where we suspected . . . Glen Ridge! And can you believe it was practically dumped in my lap by an old college friend?! Don't worry about a thing. She trusts me," Grace snickered.

"If this is a big find, I'm out of here," she told

her accomplice. "No more associate professor." The thought of the money the find could bring her excited Grace. "Now get moving! Call Smitty and make sure you two get in and out of there before word gets out."

The man on the phone was obviously not as fearless as Grace.

"What about your friend?" he asked. "Suppose she gets suspicious?"

"Just leave her to me. I'll cool out my old friend, Dee Dee," Grace assured him. "You shouldn't have any trouble finding the site. After all, the dog and the kids did all the work. They got it all staked out for us. All you have to do is get there by 3:30 tomorrow afternoon. Who's gonna be there then?"

"You never know," the man muttered.

"Hey, if somebody does show up, take care of them the way you did that creep in Colorado," Grace ordered cold-heartedly. Then she thought about Dee. "But this time, I don't want to know anything about it," she added.

CHAPTER 3

The next day, it seemed to Megan that school droned on forever. All through her classes, Megan stared absentmindedly out the window, daydreaming about the ancient Indian graveyard and the possibility of all the fame it could bring her. Megan kept picturing herself accepting great photojournalism awards in front of a crowd of adoring fans. Her mind was definitely not on her school work. How could she think about algebra when she was about to live her dream and become a professional photographer! She was so excited, she had brought her camera and bag of supplies to school. That way she didn't have to waste time going home to get the stuff. She was even wearing the camera around her neck as a constant reminder of her upcoming adventure!

As she watched the hands on the clock in her

Spanish classroom move ever so slowly toward 2:30, when school would finally let out, Megan could think of nothing but the two thousand dollars Uncle Steve had told her about. Megan fingered the camera strap around her neck lovingly. This was the most exciting day of her life!

Finally, the bell rang. Megan jumped out of her seat and ran at top speed down the hall to her locker. Quickly she turned the combination lock, opened her locker, and tossed in her books. She grabbed her vinyl camera bag and threw it over her shoulder. Then she ran right out the front door of the school without stopping to talk with her friends the way she usually did. Megan had no time to chat. She was busy starting a brand-new career! Once she got outside, Megan jumped on her bike and pedaled off in search of her future.

Back home, Will was almost as excited as Megan. He came rushing in the door like a tornado. He threw his books on the kitchen counter, opened the refrigerator door, and grabbed a quick glass of milk. Then he reached into the cookie jar for two double-chocolate, chocolate-chip cookies. After shoving them both in his mouth at the same time, he looked down at Lassie. The collie had been watching Will with fascination. She couldn't believe how fast he was moving! Will grinned at her and reached up into the cabinet for a dog biscuit. "Here's a cookie for you, girl," he laughed.

Will tossed Lassie the biscuit. The dog jumped up with her mouth open and caught the cookie in midair. She looked so much like a sea lion catching fish in a water show that Will had to laugh.

Then he looked at the clock on the oven door. 2:45! He'd better get going!

"Bye, Mom!" Will shouted behind a spray of chocolate-chip cookies as he and Lassie passed her in the family room on his way out the front door.

"What's the hurry, Will? Dashing in . . . dashing out . . ."

Will tried hard to look casual and bored. "Oh . . . nothing special," he murmured, trying to hide any shade of excitement in his voice. "I've just got to meet somebody."

"Wait just a second . . ." Dee started. She knew her son pretty well. There was more to this rush he was in than he was telling her. But before she could finish the sentence, the front door opened and then slammed, and Chris and Steve strolled into the family room.

"Hi, Dee," Chris grinned. "We just ran into an old friend of yours outside."

Dee looked behind her husband and brother-in-law. Her eyes glistened with a few happy tears. It was Grace! Sure, she was a little older and her hair was a little shorter—maybe even a little gray—but the very professional woman in the navy blue suit and red bow tie was most definitely Grace Dickenson!

"Graceless!" she shouted out. Then, embarrassed, Dee stopped herself. Her face turned bright red. "Oops! I mean . . . "

"It's okay," Grace smiled. "Graceless Grace. It was one of my nicknames in college," she explained to Chris and Steve. "It's great to see you, Dee Dee."

Will stifled a giggle. It was funny hearing someone call his mother a girlish nickname like Dee Dee.

Dee hurried to make introductions. "You've met Chris and his brother, Steve. This is our son, Will. Our daughter, Megan, isn't home right now—she's probably at an after-school club meeting as usual."

Will looked away so his mother wouldn't see his face. He knew where Megan was and she wasn't at some meeting. He decided to change the subject quickly.

"Ms. Dickenson," he said to Grace. "This is what Lassie found." His eyes filled with pride for his dog when he showed the clay pot to the professor. After all, not many dogs were junior archaeologists!

Grace picked up the pot and studied it for a second. Her heart started to race. Her wildest dreams had been fulfilled! It was real! And right about now, her two pothunting pals were driving to the site ready to dig up the rest of the goods. In just a few hours, she'd be rich!

Grace struggled to control her emotions. She couldn't act too excited, otherwise she might give herself away. She counted silently to ten to calm herself before she spoke.

"It is a Chumash medicine jar," she said professionally to Dee through carefully measured breaths. "It may be from the sixteen hundreds. Congratulations, Lassie."

Grace bent down to pat Lassie's silky brown and white head, but the collie backed away and muttered an almost human grumble of disgust. Immediately, Grace backed away in fear.

Chris looked at Lassie curiously. "I'm sorry about that, Grace," he apologized. "Lassie usually likes strangers. I guess all this excitement has gotten to her."

Lassie just stared at Grace with cold, hostile eyes.

"I'd be glad to drive you out to the site any time you want, Grace," Steve smiled at her.

"We could go today and show you right where Lassie found it," Will added excitedly, forgetting for a second that Megan was already at the field, and had told him not to mention their trek up there to anyone.

"No, I don't think it would be a good idea to

go today," she said slowly. "My associates from the college and my equipment won't be here in Glen Ridge for a few days. I think it's best we stay away until then. We don't want to attract attention."

Grace could feel her throat getting dry. That was a close one, she thought.

"Well, you just let me know when," Steve said.

"It just doesn't seem fair," Dee remarked sadly. "Digging up people's graves . . ."

"I know, but it's for science." Grace put her arm around her school chum's shoulder. "And we try to be respectful. We always return any human bones."

"And of course, it's all done under Indian supervision," Chris reminded his wife.

Grace stuttered for a second. "Oh . . . uh . . . right . . . of course."

"Grace, why don't you come see the pictures Megan took of the site," Dee suggested.

"Of course," Grace said, and gratefully followed Dee into the kitchen. Chris and Steve seem to know too much about the laws of archaeology and Indian burial sites, Grace thought irritably to herself as she followed.

"Mind if I tag along?" Steve asked as he got up and walked out behind them.

Will checked his watch. It was 3:10! He had better get moving. Megan would kill him if he was late. She would probably blame him for missing the perfect light for her shot or something.

"I've got to get going," Will told his dad.

"See ya later, Will," Chris replied.

Will turned to go but stopped in his tracks. Something was bothering him.

"I know this is silly, Dad, but uh . . . Megan was wondering about, well, you know . . . Indian curses and stuff." Actually *Will* was worried about the curses, but it was always easier to blame these things on his sister.

"Tell Megan not to worry," Chris said with a smirk. He knew it was Will who was really concerned. "But tell her to be careful. Everyone knows that if you disturb an Indian grave, the soul in it wanders forever without a home, seeking revenge."

Will grew scared. Instinctively he pulled Lassie close to him.

"I . . . uh . . . think your story's scaring Lassie," he said.

"Maybe it's a story and maybe it's not. But a long time ago, Swedish pioneers settled right here in this valley. And they dug a well on Chumash ground. People say that the Indian spirits whose graves were violated cursed the well. The Swedes got sick and their blond hair fell out in clumps."

Lassie looked up with a start.

"That's not such a bad curse . . . " Will began.

"Then they died," his father interrupted.

". . . not such a good curse either," Will continued.

"All I know is every spring, ghosts of the wandering braves cover the cottonwood plants with fine blond hairs," Chris continued.

"I've seen those plants," Will added nervously. "It does look like hair."

"A warning to the white man," Chris finished. "Never disturb our graves again."

Lassie let out an odd, sad crooning sound and moved closer to Will.

"Don't worry, Lassie," Will told his dog in a gentle tone. "Those ghosts know you didn't mean it. Anyway, it's just a story." The boy seemed to be trying to convince himself as well as the dog.

"Just in case, I'm finding another site for that warehouse," Chris told his son.

Will stood up and headed for the door. "Dad, I sure enjoyed hearing all about graves and curses and dead people. I'd love to stay for more fun talk, but I've got to get going," he joked as he closed the door behind him.

CHAPTER 4

Megan looked at her watch with disgust. 3:40! And Will still wasn't here! If her little brother didn't get to the field soon, the light would be all wrong for her photographs! And everything had to be just right for this—her first professional photography job!

Oh well, she thought irritably to herself, she couldn't wait forever. Will must have forgotten. She would bug him about it when she got home. For now, she would just have to do this without her brother's help. After all, she thought bravely to herself, real professional newspaper photographers didn't travel around with a collie and a ten-year-old sidekick!

Megan was standing on a hill just before the place where Lassie had found the ancient pot. She had her camera, three different lenses and lots of film. She was ready to take pictures of the archaeological site!

As she looked up into the sun to take a measurement of the light, she saw a ten-year-old boy riding up the hill on a black BMX bicycle. A glorious collie ran cheerfully at his side, her fuzzy tail wagging happily behind her. It was Will and Lassie! Suddenly all of Megan's professionalism fell away. She really was glad that Will and Lassie had come to help her.

"About time!" Meg said sarcastically to her brother. She was still a bit annoyed with him.

"I got stuck at the house," Will explained. "Mom's friend came to see the pot Lassie found out here, so I showed it to her. And then I had to talk to Dad about . . . something." He just couldn't tell his sister that he was scared of working near an ancient Indian grave site. She would just laugh at his fears of stirring up old ghosts. As he parked his bike in some nearby bushes, Will wondered if Megan could tell he was nervous.

He needn't have worried. Megan wasn't paying any attention to what her brother was saying. Her back was to him and she was already on her way to the site, her camera in hand. In fact, Will and Lassie had to run up the shallow, muddy hill to catch up with her.

"My first job as a professional photographer!" Megan said dreamily, her head in the clouds.

"You're going to be a great professional photographer . . . in maybe forty years," Will teased, bringing his sister back down to earth.

"I'm doing this for money," Megan retorted.

"Yeah? How much have you made so far?"

Ignoring him, Megan sat down beside the bushes near the archaeological site and began to load a roll of film into her camera.

"You know Will," she said, sounding very much like a big sister, "age has nothing to do with photography. You just need a keen eye and a sense of composition . . ."

"I guess being stuck on yourself doesn't hurt either," Will whispered, giggling, to Lassie. Lassie licked his face in response.

Will looked over at the site. He expected the peaceful field, surrounded by overgrown green bushes, to be empty. To his surprise, he saw two men. The men were wearing work clothes and had piles of picks, shovels, and polyester bags by their sides. Behind them was a small green truck.

"Hey! Somebody's over there," Will screeched, tugging on his sister's shirt. "Two men . . . and they're digging!"

Without missing a beat, Megan instinctively pushed a startled Will into the bushes with strong force. Lassie stood her ground, staring at the men. With a yank at the dog's collar, Megan pulled Lassie into the bushes with them.

"Lassie, down!" Megan commanded through clenched teeth.

Lassie reluctantly did as she was told.

"Be careful!" Meg ordered Will in a harsh whisper. "Don't let them see us!"

"What's your problem? Who are they?" Will asked her. He was annoyed. He really hated when his sister pushed him around.

Megan did not answer right away. Instead she adjusted her camera so she could study the two men through her zoom lense. The magnifying power of the camera lens brought the two figures into closer view. The men were digging rapidly into muddy ground. They threw the dirt around with absolutely no respect for the ancient burial ground. One of the men bent down and yanked a pot from the ground that seemed almost identical to the one Lassie had found. Her mind flashed back to the conversation she'd had with Uncle Steve the day before. "They're criminals . . ." he had said.

Megan tucked her hands under her arms so that Will couldn't see her shaking.

"They're pothunters!" Megan explained quickly to Will. "Grave robbers." She looked very disappointed. Her immediate thoughts were about the article. Once they looted the site, there would be nothing left for Megan to photograph. "There goes my story," she mumbled. She lowered her head and slumped her shoulders as she turned to leave quietly.

But Will was less concerned about the photographs than Megan. He just wanted to make sure the thieves did not get away with destroying an ancient Indian graveyard!

"We've got to get the police," he told his sister.

"There isn't any time," Megan said dejectedly. "They'll be gone before we get back."

"We can get their license number!"

"It won't do any good," Meg answered. "We can't prove anything."

Will pointed at the men with anger. The smaller of the two was putting yet another small round object into one of the bags. "They've found another one!" he said to his sister with disgust. He was very frustrated. His forehead crinkled and his body tightened with anger. "We can't stop them. We can't do anything!" he whined.

Lassie hated to see Will so upset. Quietly she rubbed up against his leg, trying to comfort the boy she loved. Will just wriggled his leg and shooed her off.

Meg stopped in mid step. Maybe there was something they could do. She looked through her camera one more time. At first she frowned. The men were in perfect view through the lens. And they were still hard at work stealing ancient crafts from the burial site. Then her frown shifted up into a sneaky smile.

"You're wrong, Will," she said slowly. "We can do something. We can prove they're robbing those Indian graves!"

"Sure," Will said with a little harrumph. "Who's gonna believe a couple of kids?"

"George Eastman," Megan said, holding out the camera to Will.

Will racked his brain. "Who's George . . ." he began. Then he understood his sister's plan. George Eastman! The man who founded the camera company! Megan was going to take pictures of those creeps! There is no better proof than a photograph!

"Like you always say," Will smiled at his sister, "the camera never lies!"

"Now we've got to get closer," Megan nodded. She was back in her bossy big sister mode. But this time Will was glad to follow. Sometimes his sister had some pretty smart ideas.

"Shhh! Lassie, don't say anything. Lassie, quiet!" Will commanded. Lassie obeyed and silently padded behind Will and Megan down the side of the hill and toward the two men.

As they crouched down, moving behind bushes to hide, Will smiled. "So far so good," he began. But the warning glare on Megan's face shut him up. With one look she had let him know that this was no game. This was dangerous business! From that moment on, Will followed her silently.

Finally they hit just the right spot. They were less than five feet from the pothunters, but they were shielded from their view by a gathering of high shrubs.

Peering out onto the field through her camera lens, Megan could feel the excitement building. Her heart was pounding, and her hands were still shaking, but she was not scared anymore. She felt like a newspaper photographer, taking a Pulitzer prize–winning photo in a dangerous war zone. The shrubs were like a foxhole—sort of. Professionally, Megan focused her camera and began clicking away at the scene that was unfolding before her.

Thwick! Thwick! Thwick! The shutter on the camera clicked at a rapid pace. Megan moved slightly, trying to get shots of the two men's faces, of their arms, of the stolen pots, and even a few of the pile of shovels and picks.

Finally the clicking inside the camera stopped.

"Oh nuts!" Megan growled quietly. "That was the last picture on this roll. I've got to reload."

Silently, Will reached into her camera bag and pulled out a tiny, round, plastic container of film. Megan pushed the "rewind" button on her camera.

Whirr! The noise of the film rewinding in the

camera sounded louder than usual in contrast to Lassie, Megan, and Will's silence.

The sound caused one of the two men to straighten up and look over toward the bushes that were hiding the kids.

"What was that?" he asked his nasty partner.

Panicking, Meg dug her hand into her camera bag. The rustling sound made even more noise than the rewinding film.

"There's something in those bushes," the second man said, grabbing his shovel. "C'mon!"

Carrying their shovels like weapons, the two men walked menacingly over to the bushes.

Megan and Will laid down stiff and flat on their stomachs, trying not to move. Maybe the men would look right over their heads and miss them.

"Grrr . . . " Lassie growled quietly.

Will tried to pull Lassie close to him as the men approached, but the dog didn't budge. Lassie would have none of that. She wanted to protect Will and Megan.

"Ruff! Ruff! Ruff!" When the men peered through the green leaves of the shrubs, they were greeted by the loud, ferocious, wolflike howls of an angry collie. The taller of the two men took his shovel and swung straight for Lassie's head!

Luckily the man's fear and anger caused him to lose his concentration. His aim was off, and he narrowly missed Lassie. He looked back at his friend. The very second that he turned his head, Will, Megan, and Lassie ran off through the bushes.

The two men watched them go. For a second they were relieved to have scared them off. But as he turned to go back to work, the bigger man spied the camera strap around Megan's neck.

"The girl's got a camera!" he shouted to his partner. "Get that film!"

With sharp picks and heavy shovels in their hands, the two grave robbers took off after Lassie and the kids!

CHAPTER 5

If Dee McCulloch knew the dangers her children and her dog were facing at that very moment, she might not have been in such a good mood. But because she had no idea what horrible happenings were going on at the archaeological site, she was in absolutely terrific spirits, walking around the house whistling tunes from her college days like "Good Vibrations," and "California Dreamin'."

Grace had left just an hour ago, but the visit with her college sorority "big sister" had made Dee miss her already. She only wished she'd had more time to talk about the good old days with "Graceless Grace!"

The thought of the nickname made Dee giggle a little. It was hard to think of the smooth, sophisticated college professor who had visited the house earlier this afternoon as the klutzy "Graceless Grace." Oh well, Dee thought. I suppose people really must change a bit over so much time.

"I've got a great idea," Dee said out loud, walking into the family room and interrupting her whistling to talk to Chris and Steve. "Why should Grace eat in some lonely hotel, when she can have dinner right here with us?"

"Great idea, Dee Dee," Chris teased his wife, barely holding back the laughter while he used her old nickname. "Except for one little thing. Grace never told you the name of the hotel she was staying at while she is in Glen Ridge!"

"No problem," Dee answered. "I'll just call the college and ask. I'm sure this Indian project is so important to Grace that she'll be checking in with her department all the time. I'm certain someone at her office will know where she is staying."

Dee picked up the phone and dialed the number of the college. It was still written on the pad on her desk from her call the day before.

After three rings the Archaeology Department's secretary answered the phone.

"Hi! I'm Dee McCulloch, a friend of Grace Dickenson's. I was wondering if you could tell me the name of the hotel Grace is staying at here in Glen Ridge."

The secretary seemed confused. "Glen Ridge?" she repeated after Dee.

"Yes, you know, the place where the Indian relics were found? Grace is here to check them out and . . ."

The secretary broke in before Dee could finish what she was saying. Steve and Chris watched with concern as Dee's facial expression turned from joy to total confusion as the conversation continued. When the secretary finally finished, Dee said in a dazed voice, "That's strange. I must have misunderstood . . . Thank you."

She hung up the phone and stared helplessly at her husband. "The University doesn't know anything about our find," she said slowly. "Grace told them she was going back east for a wedding. They have no record of any workers being sent up here to begin any archaeological dig." She sat on the couch and looked at Chris.

"Uh oh," Steve began earnestly.

"Uh oh what?" Chris asked his brother anxiously.

"You know, I thought she seemed a little rattled when you mentioned consulting the Indians about digging at the site . . . " Steve thought out loud.

Chris got on his brother's wavelength right away. "You're right," he added. "She did just sort of mumble something and get all uncomfortable."

"What are you two babbling about?" Dee questioned. She was getting irritated.

Steve turned to Dee. He did not want to hurt his sister-in-law's feelings but he had to tell her what he suspected.

"I have a hunch that right now, your friend 'Graceless' is out there looting the place," he said gently, but with an unmistakably urgent firmness in his voice.

Dee shot her brother-in-law an angry glare. This was, after all, one of her oldest and dearest friends he was talking about. "I can't believe that!"

Chris put his arm around his wife's shoulder and tried to comfort her. "Maybe you don't want to believe it."

Dee sat quietly, reviewing the events of the past few days in her head. She began to recall some strange occurrences—Grace's request that Dee not say anything to anyone about the find, Steve's description of dangerous pothunters, Grace's visit to the house, Lassie's rude reaction to Grace, this last phone call to the college, the kids . . . Suddenly she panicked!

"Chris . . . the kids? Where are the kids," she cried, the lines in her forehead burrowing with concern. "This afternoon Will was in quite a hurry! He wouldn't tell me where he was heading. And Megan didn't even stop home after school.

You don't think . . . I mean . . . they wouldn't go out there alone."

Chris was already standing up and heading out the door to the family 4×4.

"Don't bet on it," he said as he looked outside into the glaring sunshine. "We'd better hurry up and drive over there!"

CHAPTER 6

As the 4×4 raced quickly down the highway, Lassie, Megan, and Will were doing some racing of their own—down the grass-covered shallow hill that blocked the ancient Indian burial grounds from the modern three-lane highway that bordered the warehouse site.

Without breaking her stride, Megan turned her head quickly to take a look behind her. The men were still closing in on them. If only she, Will, and Lassie could get to the highway before they grabbed them, she thought, maybe a passing car could pick them up and take them to safety.

"HEY!" a joyous, breathless scream from Will broke into Megan's thoughts.

Megan stopped suddenly as her eyes followed the direction of Will's pointed forefinger. There, at the bottom of the hill, was a bright red four-door sedan. A woman about her mother's age, dressed in a pair of overalls and a checkered flannel shirt stepped out of the car and looked out toward the hill.

"That's Grace—mom's friend," Will shouted to Megan.

"We've got . . . to get . . . to her," Megan panted to him. Her heart was pounding hard against her chest. Will doubled his speed down the hill toward Grace Dickenson.

"Ruff! Ruff! Ruff! Ruff!" Lassie barked a fierce warning call to Will. She did not trust this woman. Something about Grace seemed wrong to Lassie. The dog had no way of knowing what type of criminal Grace really was, but the collie's instincts told her that Dee McCulloch's old pal was not who she claimed to be. Under ordinary circumstances, Will would have understood immediately that Lassie was trying to warn him about the true identity of "good old Graceless Grace." But Will was too scared to listen to his beloved collie.

"RUFF! RUFF! RUFF! RUFF!" Lassie growled even louder from deep in her throat. Megan ignored the mighty collie's cries, too. Instead, she tried to follow her brother's lead down the hill toward the woman who had been her mother's idol in college. But before Megan could take two steps in Will's direction, the smaller of the two grave robbers grabbed Megan from behind! She let out a screech of terror as his arm squeezed tightly around her waist! Megan shook in terror. The creep was squeezing the air right out of her!

"HARUFF!" Lassie let out the loudest yelp she had ever barked. Then, with ever increasing speed, she ran toward the man and, with the look of a wild wolf in her eyes, took a flying leap toward Megan's captor! She grabbed the bottom of his shirt in her sharp white teeth and, with the simple turn of her powerful, noble head, the collie yanked the evil thief away from Megan. The collie pulled at the man with such intense force he was thrown off guard. Lassie watched as he toppled in a heap of twisted arms and legs down the pale green grass of the hill.

"WILL!" Megan called out to her brother in a panic. Will stopped and turned back toward his sister.

"Think fast!" she shouted to her brother. Then, using all of what was left of her strength, Megan threw a small gray and black plastic cannister of film in Will's direction.

Will reached out and grabbed the cannister in mid flight. He cocked his head, smiled a glowing grin, and held the cannister up so his sister could see that he had, indeed, caught the film. Then he took off after Grace in the hope of finding safety in her car.

Unfortunately, Megan was not the only one to see Will hold up the film cannister. The larger of the two crooks had caught a glimpse of it, too.

"Get up!" he ordered his fallen partner in a loud, gravelly voice. "He's got the film! Get that boy!"

The smaller man scrambled to his feet and followed his accomplice who was already on a wild chase down the hill after Will!

"RUFF! RUFF!" Lassie barked wildly at the men. But before she could rush off to Will's aid, Megan grabbed Lassie in a loving bear hug around the thick white hair that protected her neck.

"Hide girl! Hide!" Megan ordered the collie. Then she opened her arms and set the dog free from her grasp.

Lassie looked longingly at Will, who at this moment was less than a few feet ahead of two vicious criminals. She wanted desperately to help him. Still, an order from any member of the family had to be obeyed.

"Lassie, hide! Run!" Megan ordered again, with a new sense of urgency in her voice. With one last sorrowful look at Will, the brave collie darted into the brush on the side of the hill.

Finally, after what seemed forever, Will reached Grace's car. The men were close behind.

"Hurry!" Will whispered out between short, deep breaths. "We've got to get in the car," he gulped. "They're after this," he added, handing her the cannister of film his sister had thrown to him.

Will was exhausted. He leaned up against the red sedan and breathed heavily. His face was red and bathed in sweat.

"Thank you," Grace said to him, looking at the cannister of film with a sinister grin.

SCREECH! The shiny black McCulloch 4×4 skidded to a halt behind the red car. Will looked over with a start. Then he smiled. He had never been so glad to see anyone in his life!

Chris and Steve jumped out of the 4×4 and ran toward the two men who had been chasing the kids. Steve jumped right onto the smaller man and wrestled him to the ground. Chris took on the bigger man and with one powerful punch, knocked him to the ground as well.

"Thank goodness you're here," Grace smiled sweetly at Dee. "These horrible men . . ." she began.

" . . . are working for you, Grace," Dee broke in, finishing the sentence.

But Grace was not ready to give up on her lie. "I don't know what you're talking about," she said in a voice that was a bit too sweet. Dee could not help noticing that Grace looked a lot like a trapped animal as she squirmed uncomfortably and kicked at the ground.

"Come on, Grace, give it up," Dee continued. "Next I suppose you are going to try and tell us that these two . . . " she pointed at the two captured pothunters, " . . . are university professors." Her eyes grew misty when she looked at her old friend. "Grace, you were such an idealist," she said sadly.

"Twenty years ago," Grace snapped back at Dee. Then she looked at her two accomplices. "It doesn't matter, guys," she smiled. "They can't prove anything!"

Will looked at Grace with amazement. Suddenly he understood. "You're one of them!" he shrieked.

"One of whom?" Grace snarled at the boy.

"We've got the proof right there," he said, pointing to the cannister of film in her hand.

Grace laughed a quick, deep laugh. "Oh, you mean, this," she said sarcastically as she opened the cannister and exposed all the film to the bright sunlight. The pictures were ruined! Then she crumpled the film into a little ball and threw it right at Dee's face!

"Sorry, Dee Dee," she laughed. "No photographs, no case!"

Dee looked helplessly at Chris. Just then, Megan ran up beside her mother. "Lassie, come!" she shouted into the bushes.

Obediently, Lassie ran to the girl. Megan bent down and placed her hand under the collie's chin.

"Give, Lassie."

Everyone stared as Lassie opened her mouth and dropped a small gray and black plastic film cannister into Megan's waiting hand.

"Good girl," Megan grinned, patting the collie's brown and white side with her free hand. Then she held the cannister up to her mother with a triumphant smile.

"Mom, here are the real photographs," she said simply. "We've got a case," she added, staring right into Grace's startled eyes.

Dee rushed to hug her quick-thinking daughter.

"Megan, honey. You took pictures? Do you realize the danger you were in?"

Will sided up to his mother for a hug, too. "What about me?" he demanded. "Megan gave me the wrong film. I was a decoy!" He looked at his sister angrily. "You let them chase me!"

"What can I say? It worked!" Megan giggled.

Uncle Steve looked triumphantly at his niece and nephew. "Now we have a story!" he announced.

EPILOGUE

Chris and Steve agreed to keep watch over the three criminals—with a little help from Lassie. The purebred collie's wolflike glare, growls, and sharp, gleaming white teeth were like an insurance policy. No one would try to run with Lassie threatening to attack. So Dee and the kids took the film and, in no time at all, Dee had driven the 4×4 down the road to a small gas station and called the Glen Ridge police. It took less than five minutes for three police cars to come to the site, their sirens blaring down the road. Dee looked away sadly as the police handcuffed her old college chum and the two men, read them their rights, and helped them bend down to climb into the backseat of a police car. The McCullochs followed the police cars into town and over to the police station, where the criminals were formally charged with robbing an Indian gravesite.

Although she was proud of her part in the capture of the three grave robbers, Megan was less than thrilled with the prospect of having to give up her beloved photographs to the police. They would be used as official evidence against the three criminals.

The next evening, Megan was still disappointed about losing the chance to be a professional photographer. She watched through teary eyes as a news reporter told the story of the robbery attempt at the Indian graveyard. Megan snapped off the evening news and sat angrily on the couch next to her mother. She kept her arms folded tightly against her chest.

"Meg, you did get your pictures on TV," Dee said gently. The local news station had gotten permission from the McCullochs and the police to show Megan's pictures on their evening broadcast.

"Yeah. What's two thousand dollars when I got this 'Newshound' T-shirt from Channel Nine," Megan moaned sarcastically, throwing the shirt on the floor.

"Meg, this is not about money," her mother said slowly, trying not to be annoyed with Megan's obvious selfishness. "Your film saved an important part of history."

"I guess that was kind of fun," Megan said

with a grin. "And it was exciting running after those thieves." She looked sadly at her mother. "Oh . . . I'm sorry about your friend," she added.

"So am I. And I'm sorry you didn't get to do the magazine article. But it's a big story. That's why they are sending out their own staff people. Remember, Uncle Steve missed out, too. Someday, honey, you're going to be a professional photographer."

"Someday," Megan muttered.

Megan and Dee looked up as the door slammed and Will, still muddy and sweaty from his after-school soccer practice, ran excitedly into the room.

"Hey Megan! I've got a problem. The soccer team needs a picture for the yearbook."

"So what?"

"The photographer wants fifty bucks!" Will explained.

"You want me to do it for nothing?" Megan frowned.

"Maybe twenty?" Will answered.

Megan looked happily at her mother. "If I got paid, you know what that would make me?"

Dee nodded with a smile. "A professional photographer."

Will flushed. "Yeah . . . well . . . why not . . . you're good enough." He was embarrassed. Why did his sister have to make everything into a major case? Will charged up the steps to change, Lassie following close behind.

"Hey, Will," Megan shouted after him. "Thanks!"